GLORIA the GLADIATOR

FUSION

'Gloria the Gladiator'
An original concept by Katie Dale
© Katie Dale 2024

Illustrated by Clari Cabral

Published by MAVERICK ARTS PUBLISHING LTD
Suite 1, Hillreed House, 54 Queen Street,
Horsham, West Sussex, RH13 5AD
© Maverick Arts Publishing Limited September 2024
+44 (0)1403 256941

A CIP catalogue record for this book is available at the British Library.

ISBN 978-1-83511-038-6

Printed in India

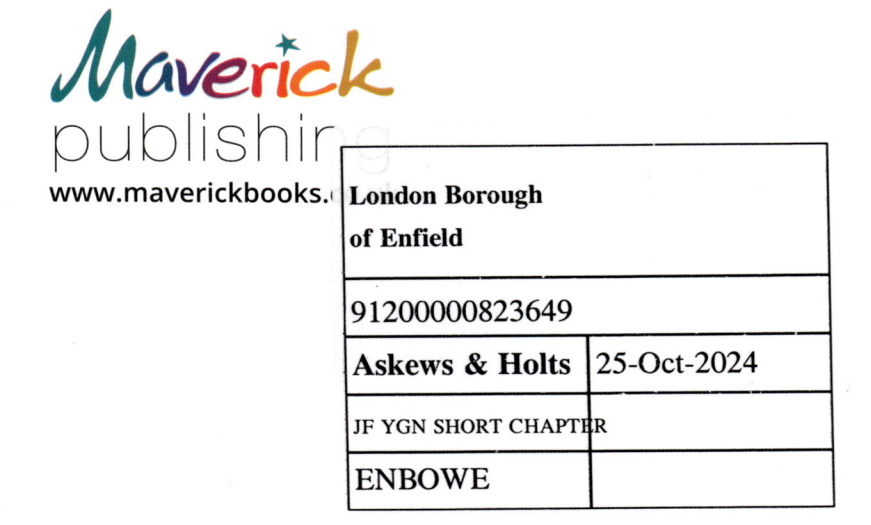

www.maverickbooks.co.uk

London Borough of Enfield	
91200000823649	
Askews & Holts	25-Oct-2024
JF YGN SHORT CHAPTER	
ENBOWE	

GLORIA the GLADIATOR

Written by Katie Dale

Illustrated by Clari Cabral

Chapter 1
Girls Can't Be Gladiators

CRASH! CLANG! SMASH!

The deafening sound of metal on metal echoed around the courtyard.

Gloria dropped her basket of laundry and raced outside, her heart beating wildly. Was someone in trouble?!

But as she reached the courtyard, she suddenly heard the sound of laughter… Her brothers' laughter.

She smiled and watched enviously as they circled each other. Their swords clashed together, with sunlight glittering off the blades. Gloria sighed. She'd give anything to join in. But girls weren't allowed to be gladiators…

CLASH!

SMASH!

Suddenly...

Beat you again, Adrian!

It's not fair! Your sword's bigger than mine, Marcus.

A bad gladiator blames his sword!

What would you know? Girls can't fight!

Bigger isn't always better. A lighter sword can be more useful...

If only you knew...

Every night, Gloria practised in secret...

SWISH! SWOOSH!

YES!

Gloria!

Father!

"What on earth were you doing with that sword?" Gloria's father demanded, snatching it off her.

"Um..." Gloria thought quickly. "Cleaning it!" she fibbed.

"That's very kind of you," her father sighed. "I know your brothers are both very keen to look and perform their best in their trial battle tomorrow."

Gloria's ears pricked up. "Trial battle?"

"Yes, they're hoping to be picked to take part in the Emperor's Young Gladiators Tournament—the prize is a bag of gold!" Her father beamed. "You have no idea how much that money could help our family. Times are hard, my dear."

"Then I'll polish this sword until it gleams!" Gloria said, reaching for it.

"No!" her father said, putting it away. "Promise me you will never touch it again!" he demanded. "Swords are dangerous—you could hurt yourself."

Gloria sighed. "Yes, Father."

"Good girl." He smiled, hugging her. "Now, don't stay up too long, my dear. It's late."

Chapter 2
The Golden Gladiator

"Give me more bread, Gloria!" Adrian cried at breakfast the next morning. "I'll need lots of energy for our trial battle!"

"Don't eat *too* much or you'll be too slow!" Marcus teased.

"Too slow?" Adrian scoffed. "Bet I can beat you there!"

"You're on!" Marcus cried.

Gloria sighed as they raced away, wishing for the hundredth time she could go and fight too.

"I'm going out for the day too," her father said. "I won't be back till supper. Have a good day, Gloria."

Gloria sighed again as she cleared the breakfast plates. Then suddenly, she had an idea…

Bingo! Father's old armour!
Just need to disguise it a bit...
Perfect! Now I can join the trial battle without being recognised. But how will I fight without a sword...?
Yes!

Who's that?
And what kind of a weapon is that?! Haha!
CRASH!
An effective one!
BASH!
A highly effective—and very original—one! Very impressive. I'll see you at my tournament, Golden Gladiator!
Yes!

Chapter 3
The Tournament

That evening, Gloria couldn't keep the smile off her face. As she served supper, all her brothers could talk about was the mysterious Golden Gladiator who had been invited to fight in the tournament by the Emperor himself.

"You should have seen him, Father!" Marcus cried. "He was so quick and skilful, Adrian didn't stand a chance!"

"He caught me off-guard, that's all!" Adrian insisted. "I'll get another chance to fight him in the tournament. I'll be ready for him next time."

Gloria grinned. She was so glad both her brothers had also been invited to compete—after all, that way her family stood a better chance of winning the bag of gold!

"Who was he?" their father asked.

"That's just it—no one knows!" Marcus cried. "He didn't give his name. He never said a word! But he was dressed all in yellow so the Emperor called him the 'Golden Gladiator'."

Her father raised an eyebrow. "Very mysterious."

Gloria grinned. How she wanted to tell them it was her! She'd love to see the look on their faces! But if she did, they wouldn't let her fight, would they? No, first she had to prove herself. Prove that she was just as good as her brothers—*better* even! She couldn't wait for the tournament!

But that night in bed, Gloria's excitement turned to nerves. What if her father was really angry when he found out? What if she really *did* get hurt? Who would look after her family then? Her brothers had never even *looked* at a broom, and her father's previous attempts at cooking had been... well, not very edible. Gloria bit her lip. Should she back out?

But then... what if she won the gold? It could feed her family for months! That settled it. She *had* to fight!

On the day of the tournament...
Gulp!
BASH!
SMASH!
CRASH!
Ouch!
Next up... the Golden Gladiator!
Double gulp!
Triple gulp!

"Would you like a sword, Gladiator?"

"Tempting... but I promised Father I wouldn't touch another sword."

The fight began.

Gloria dived under his legs...

"Gulp - he's HUGE!"

...disarmed the gladiator...

...and won!

SWIPE!

"Next up... Adrian the Agile!"

"You won't beat me this time, Golden Gladiator!" Adrian growled, raising his sword and lunging at Gloria. Gloria darted and dodged his blows, so he swung his sword through thin air.

"Coward!" Adrian yelled angrily.

Can't catch me! Gloria thought, grinning as she leapt out of his reach.

"Stop running away and fight me!" Adrian panted as she whirled away again. Gloria smiled. He was getting tired. He must have had too much for breakfast again!

He raised his sword again and she swiftly side-stepped, but—oh no!—she tripped over a rock! She tumbled to the ground, grazing her knee as she desperately clung on to her stick.

"Ouch!" Gloria yelped before she could stop herself.

Adrian frowned, his head on one side.

Oh no! Gloria thought, panicking. *Did he hear me shout out? Has he recognised my voice?* She braced herself as he stepped closer. Was it all over?

Chapter 4
Brother vs. Sister

"I've got you now, Golden Gladiator!" Adrian grinned triumphantly as he loomed over her. "Whoever you are!"

Gloria didn't know whether to feel relieved or worried. Her brother clearly *hadn't* recognised her—but he might be about to knock her out of the tournament!

"I can't wait to see who you really are, you coward!" Adrian cried, his sword glinting in the sunlight as it swung towards her.

That gave Gloria an idea! She rolled onto her knees and jabbed her stick upwards, but not at Adrian's sword...

Hey!
Cheat!
That's not fair!
The rules say the winner is the first to disarm their opponent! The Golden Gladiator wins again!

Next up, Marcus the Mighty!
CLASH!
BASH!
The Golden Gladiator wins!

It seemed like Gloria was on a roll...

WOO! HURRAY!

Gloria had never felt so alive! Every time she won, the crowd's cheers grew louder and louder—even Marcus and Adrian and her father were cheering for her now! Her heart pounded with excitement as she ducked, darted, jabbed and parried, defeating every opponent she faced. Each boy who entered the arena was bigger and stronger than her, but Gloria was swifter and nimbler and cleverer. Try as they might, they just couldn't keep up with her.

Finally, there was only one opponent left.

"THE WINNER OF THE NEXT BATTLE WINS THE TOURNAMENT!" the announcer proclaimed.

Gloria's skin tingled with excitement. Could she actually *win* the whole tournament? Win the bag of gold for her family, solve her father's money worries, and finally prove to them all that she could fight? Prove to *everyone* that girls were just as good as boys? That they shouldn't just be stuck at home, doing chores?

Then the last gladiator entered the arena...

"Our last contender is **HORATIO THE HUGE!**"

No kidding... Gulp!

Yes!

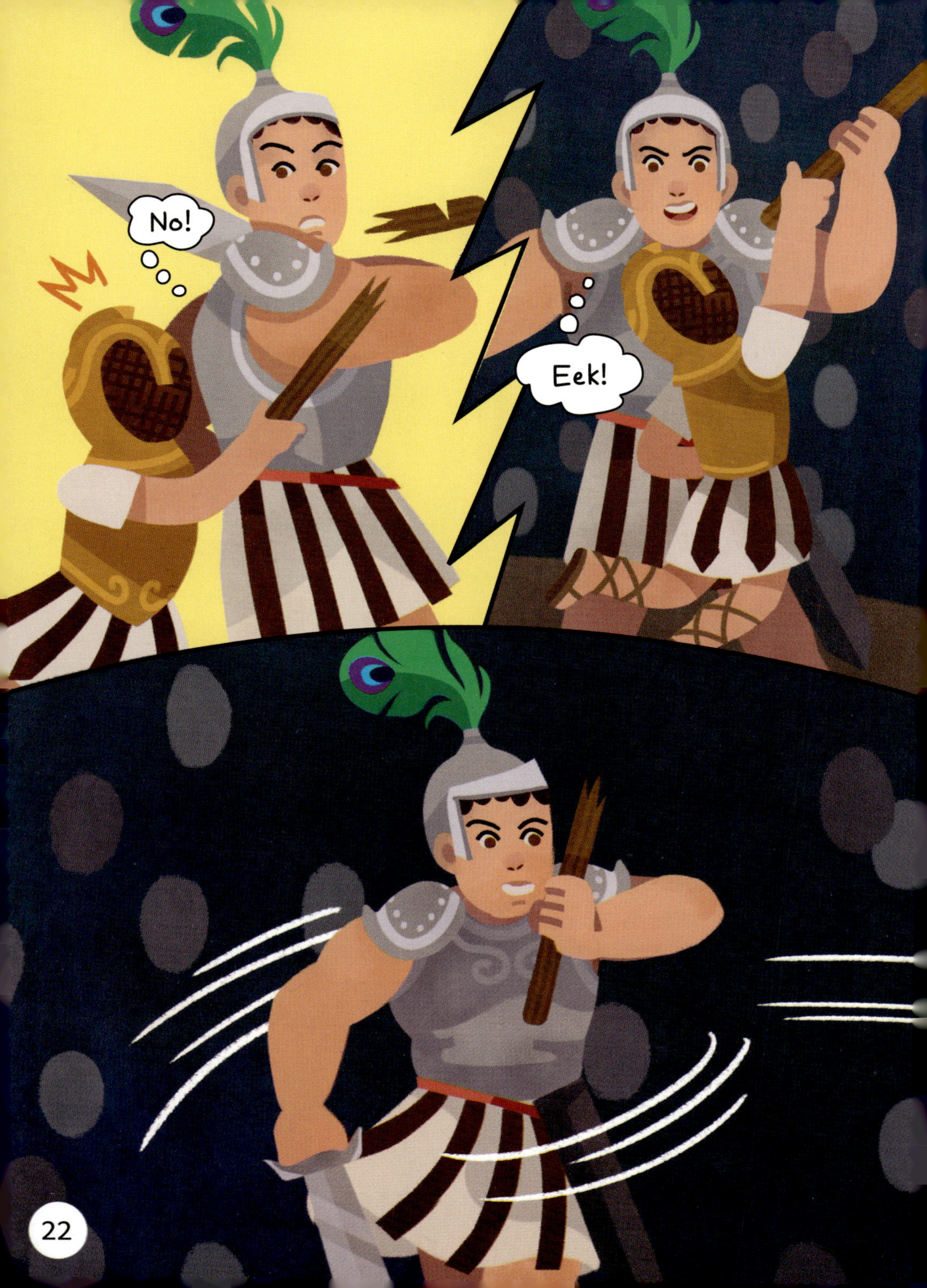
No!
Eek!

Gloria tumbled to the ground, bashing her knee and bruising her arm, but nothing hurt more than her heart. She stared at her empty hand as hot tears stung her eyes. She had let go of her stick...

"Horatio the Huge is our winner!" the announcer proclaimed.

The crowd's cheers filled the arena, and Gloria felt all her hopes and dreams fizzle away. She had lost the battle, lost the tournament, lost her one and only chance to prove herself.

It was over.

Chapter 5
The Truth

"Congratulations, Horatio!" the Emperor cried and the crowd cheered again. "Please, come here to receive your bag of gold!"

Gloria sighed heavily as she watched Horatio race across the arena, his fancy armour gleaming and the peacock feather on his helmet bobbing in the breeze.

I bet he doesn't even need the money, Gloria thought bitterly as Horatio lifted the heavy sack above his head triumphantly. He was so strong, but Gloria barely even had the strength to pick herself up off the ground. She felt like such a failure.

But then...

Golden Gladiator, come and receive your prize!

25

"Congratulations! Well deserved!"

"A bag of silver? Yes! This will feed my family for weeks!"

It was the best moment of Gloria's life! Until...

CLATTER!

Gloria froze. She hardly dared to breathe as the whole arena fell silent and she felt everybody's gaze pinned on her. Then one voice pierced the silence.

"Gloria...?" her father said, his voice trembling with disbelief. Gloria's heart beat fast as she turned to look at him and her brothers.

"Yes, Father," she said, swallowing hard, trying to read his wide-eyed expression. Was he impressed? Or ashamed? He opened his mouth again but, before he could say another word, the Emperor spoke.

"Our Golden Gladiator has a voice at last," he said. "And a name. One I would never have guessed." He raised an eyebrow. "Gloria?"

Gloria nodded, her cheeks blazing, the bag of silver heavy in her hands. Would the Emperor even let her keep it, now he knew she was a girl? Girls weren't allowed to be gladiators, after all...

"Gloria the gladiator..." the Emperor continued, frowning. "Who trained you?"

"No one," Gloria admitted. "I trained myself, in secret."

The Emperor's eyebrows shot up. "In secret? You mean even your family had no idea?"

Gloria shook her head. "No one knew."

"Really?" the Emperor said. "And tell me, why do you use a stick instead of a sword?"

"I used to use a sword, but my father found me with it and made me promise not to touch one ever again," she explained, glancing at her father. "He said it was too dangerous."

"So you are honourable and trustworthy, as well as a skilled warrior?" The Emperor smiled. "You must come and help train students at my Gladiator School!"

Everyone gasped. Gloria's jaw dropped.

"I will pay you well, and my army will train you to be a real warrior." The Emperor beamed. "That is, if your father will allow you to use a sword again?"

Gloria's father smiled and nodded, and everyone cheered. Gloria's heart felt like it would burst with happiness. She'd earn enough to feed her family *and* be allowed to fight?!

The Emperor beamed at Gloria. "After all, you've proven that there's no reason why girls shouldn't be gladiators too—perhaps there'll even be a female Emperor one day!"

Everyone cheered. Gloria's father and brothers were loudest of all!

When they got home, Gloria's father gave her a huge hug. "I'm so proud of you, Gloria!" he cried.

"Me too!" cried Marcus, joining the hug.

"Me three!" Adrian grinned, squeezing them all tight. "But when did you have time to train, Gloria? You always seemed so busy doing chores!"

"Which Adrian and I will both do now you're a professional gladiator teacher!" Marcus added quickly. "If you'll teach us some of your tricks?"

"Of course!" Gloria smiled. "Actually, that's *exactly* how I trained!" She threw a carrot in the air, grabbed Adrian's sword, and sliced it before it fell. Her brothers gasped.

"Chores are going to be fun!" Adrian cried.

Everyone laughed.

The End

WHAT NEXT?

Did you enjoy this Fusion Reader? If you are looking for more, the Maverick Reading Scheme is a bright, attractive range of books with plenty of stories for everyone. All titles are book-banded for guided reading to the industry standard and edited by a leading educational consultant.

MAVERICK FUSION READERS

To view the whole Maverick Reading Scheme, visit our website at www.maverickearlyreaders.com

Or scan the QR code to view our scheme instantly!